To Nanny,

Thank you for always telling us your wonderful stories. Here's one you told us, with a twist, so we can continue to tell it to your great grandchildren and beyond.

HELENA

Written by

Christina Alice Morris

Helena was playing by Crosby beach with her dog, Rusty.

It was nearly time to leave, her shoes were sandy and dusty.

She loved the beach but preferred not to swim.

She realised that she couldn't see Rusty so she

called to him.

"Rusty, we're home. Now go to your bed."

She was a bit late home and she started to dread.

Her Mummy wasn't worried, she was staring away,

She looked sad and had something to say.

To the wireless radio, her mummy had a listen,

Which is why her eyes had begun to glisten.

"Helena, there is a reason I am sad,

We are going to war and war is very bad."

War is when people fight,

But in our house, we think it's not right.

Your brothers and father will have to go,

And when they come back, I do not know.

"To our family friend's house,
you will go to stay.
I do not know how
long you will be away.
I will take you to
the ferry station.
This is for your safety.
It's called evacuation."

Unlike her school friends, Helena knew –
The place that she was being evacuated to.
Off she traveled to the Isle of Man by sea,
Wondering what her future would be.

The ferry to the Isle of Man felt long.

Without her siblings to play and sing a song.

Without her mummy and daddy's hand to hold,

Helena was curious what would unfold.

Her family friends were very kind.

Home was always at the forefront of her mind.

Her window looked onto the beach,

She thought of her family, who were out of reach.

At night, Helena could hear the whale's song.

She imagined going home on a whale's back, riding along.

Back home to be with her family to dance.

She couldn't bear to think of her brothers in France.

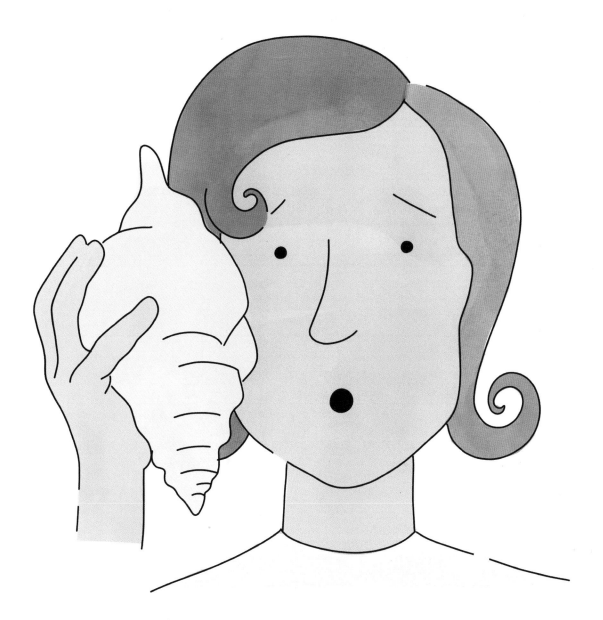

One day on the beach she picked up a shell.

She listened to what it had to tell.

She put the white seashell to her ear.

"Listen to the whales" it whispered "and do not fear".

That night, Helena listened out,

She could hear the whales all about.

Whales don't have a country or believe in war.

They live for peace off the shore.

Helena closed her eyes hoping she could hear.

Had that shell really spoken in her ear?

"Are my parents, brothers and sisters OK?"

"Yes, Helena. Don't dismay."

Helena told her host family's son about the whales.

She worried he would think that she was telling tales.

Though he couldn't wait to hear,

The reassuring whales that came near.

They stayed up one night when their host was in bed,

They asked about her mummy and the whale said...

"She misses you all and she is very upset"

"I should go home. I'm not meant to go back yet."

She left her hosts on the isle,

She knew the ferry would take a while.

She was anxious about bombs and the dangers of war,

She knew home wouldn't be like it was before.

On the ferry she heard the whales singing happily.

She was to be reunited with their family.

Helena's mummy was so happy to have her home.

She would no longer

feel all alone.

The war continued for six years,

There was lots of wondering and still some tears,

The happiest day they had ever known,

Was when Daddy, Gerard and Alf returned home.

Helena knew that they would never believe the tale,

That she returned home because she spoke to a whale.

She was only young but she promised her heart,

That family was very important and this wisdom she would impart.

Helena did indeed become a nanny to seven girls and boys.

She was a wonderful storyteller and bought them lovely toys.

She would recite poems and take them the zoo.

She was a lovely nanny, that was true.

Helena taught her family the importance of the clan,

Siblings, cousins, uncles, aunts and Nan,

Every Christmas all her descendants would meet,

Great dinner, wonderful games. Always a treat.

You can't choose your family but Helena felt like she had.

She had learnt so much from missing her dad.

Helena lived her whole life by the seaside.

Sometimes, still, hearing whales beyond the tide.

Printed in Poland
by Amazon Fulfillment
Poland Sp. z o.o., Wrocław

85571733R00016